PLEASE WASH
YOUR HANDS
BEFORE YOU READ ME
AND KEEP ME CLEAN

10/97

GAYLORD F

The Surprise
in the Wardrobe

Val Willis

Pictures by
John Shelley

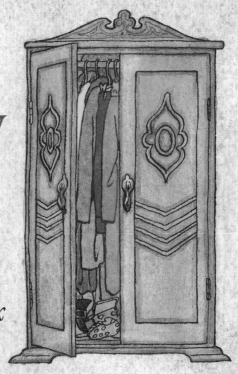

Farrar, Straus & Giroux
New York

Bobby Bell had a surprise and the surprise was in his wardrobe. Bobby could not wait to get to school. He wanted to tell his teacher, Miss Potts, about his surprise.

Bobby met his friend Peter Drew on the way to school. When they arrived, Jenny Wood was in the playground. She was holding a big cardboard box with holes in the lid.
"I have a wonderful surprise," Bobby said to Jenny.

"I've got a better surprise than you," said Jenny Wood. "Look!" She opened the box and there was a rabbit, munching a lettuce leaf. "My surprise is better than that," said Bobby. "Do you want to hear?" "No," said Jenny, stroking her rabbit.

Bobby saw little Helen Wells in the classroom.
"I've got a tremendous surprise," he said.
"So have I," whispered little Helen Wells. "It's my birthday today."
She opened her desk and showed Bobby a birthday cake on a
silver plate.

"It's for us all to share at playtime," she said.
"But don't you want to hear about my surprise?" said Bobby.
"Not really," whispered little Helen Wells.
Miss Potts came into the classroom.
"I've got a surprise," Bobby said to Miss Potts. "It's fantastic."

"Be quiet Bobby," said Miss Potts, "and go to your seat."
"Now, class," she went on, "we shall be having a new girl
joining us tomorrow. I expect you all to look after her and

help her as much as you can."

"I'll bring my surprise tomorrow, too," said Bobby. "It's in my wardrobe."

After school, Bobby ran home and went straight up to his bedroom. He opened his wardrobe door. A witch was hanging up on a coat hanger. Bobby lifted her down. The witch straightened her hat and sat on Bobby's bed.

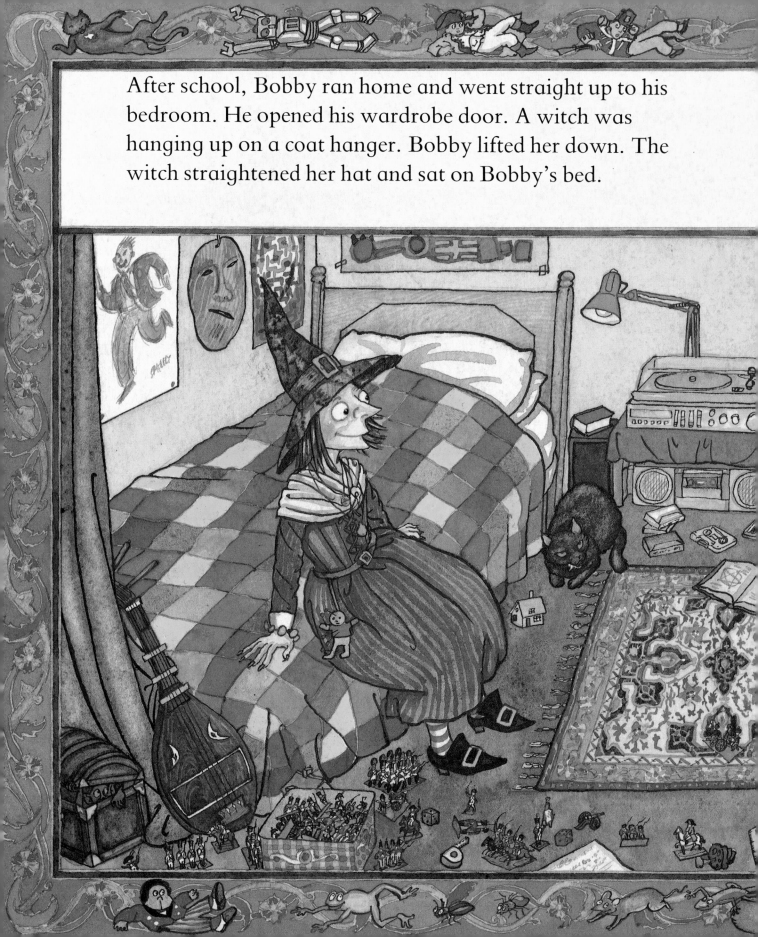

"I'm taking you to school with me tomorrow," said Bobby.
The witch grinned and pulled a bottle of green nail polish from
the pocket of her black dress. She began to paint her nails.
"I'd better put you away," said Bobby. "It's my tea time."
And he hung the witch back up in the wardrobe.

The next day after breakfast, Bobby took the witch out of the wardrobe. She looked a bit of a mess. Her dress was creased, her hat was bent, and her hair stuck out all over.

Bobby handed her his hairbrush and she put it in her pocket.
"Come on," said Bobby, "or we'll be late for school."

The witch took her broomstick from the umbrella stand in the hall. Outside in the garden, Bobby climbed on the broomstick behind the witch and they whizzed up into the air.

They had so much fun that they didn't get to school until it was nearly lunchtime.

Bobby and the witch landed in the playground. They walked over to Jenny Wood, who was jumping rope. Jenny Wood saw the witch and dropped her jump rope.

The witch picked up the jump rope and did some very fancy steps with it. Bobby was impressed.
"I told you," he said to Jenny Wood.

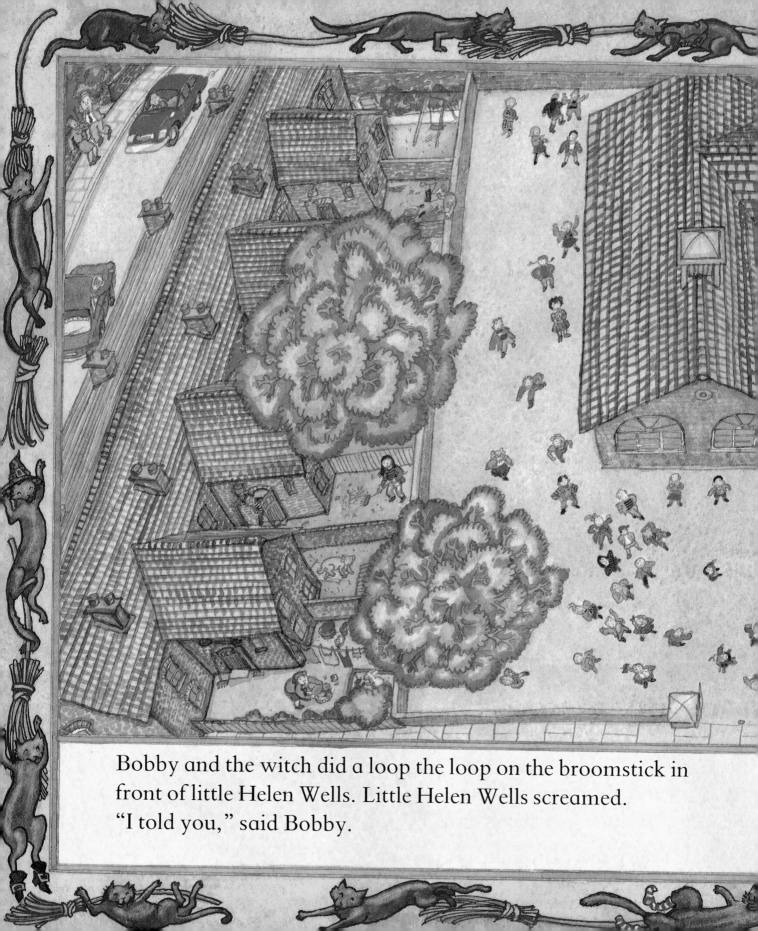

Bobby and the witch did a loop the loop on the broomstick in front of little Helen Wells. Little Helen Wells screamed.
"I told you," said Bobby.

The bell rang for lunch. Bobby took the witch into the lunchroom.
Bobby smiled at Miss Potts and waited.
"Ah," said Miss Potts. "I'm glad you've decided to come at
last. I see you've brought the new girl, too."

"What new girl?" said Bobby.
Miss Potts took no notice.
"Go and sit next to Jenny Wood," she said to the witch.

Jenny Wood made a face.
"I don't want to sit next to her, Miss Potts. She's a mess."
"Don't fuss, Jenny," said Miss Potts.

Jenny sat down and stood up again.
"What's the matter *now*, Jenny?" said Miss Potts.
"Someone put a hedgehog on my chair," said Jenny.
"Was it you, Bobby Bell?" said Miss Potts.

"No, Miss Potts," said Bobby. "It must have been the witch."
"Don't be rude, Bobby," said Miss Potts.
"Time to line up for lunch," said Miss Potts.
"Bobby Bell, you look after the new girl."

Bobby and the witch stood in the line, waiting to be served by Mrs. Fry, the school cook.

"Stew and cabbage. Yuk," said the witch.

"Don't be rude, Bobby Bell," said Mrs. Fry.

Mrs. Fry glared at the witch and waved her ladle in the air.
Bobby and the witch took their plates to their table and sat
down with the rest of the class.
"Cabbage and stew," said Bobby. "Yuk, yuk, yuk."

The witch winked at Bobby and the table was covered with french fries, hot dogs, and baked beans. Bobby's class cheered. Jenny Wood said she preferred stew and cabbage.

The witch looked at Bobby and winked again. A fat green frog jumped on Jenny Wood's plate. Jenny Wood screamed loud and long. Fat green frogs appeared all over the lunchroom.

The class held its breath. Mrs. Fry waved her ladle, glared, and called out, "Pudding." "Prunes and sago," said the witch. "Yuk, yuk, yuk." "I shan't tell you again, Bobby Bell," said Mrs. Fry.

Bobby and the witch took their plates to their table and sat down.
The witch winked at Bobby again. The table was covered with
cakes, candies, ice cream, and soda pop. The class cheered again.
Peter Drew said he preferred sago and prunes.

The witch snapped her fingers. A fat hairy spider swung down from the ceiling and hung over Peter Drew's plate. Bats, beetles, and bugs flew and crawled all over the lunchroom. Mrs. Fry glared.

"There's always trouble when Bobby Bell's around," she said.

Mrs. Fry waved her ladle. "Bobby Bell, you'd better clear up my dining room before Miss Potts sees it."

"Don't worry," whispered the witch. "I got you into this mess and I'll get you out of it." She snapped her fingers and all the frogs, beetles, and bats disappeared in a swirl of green mist.

"I'm going back to your wardrobe now," the witch said to Bobby. "I've had enough school for one day."

"Thanks for your help," said Bobby.

"Don't mention it," said the witch. And she hopped on her broomstick and flew off.